THIS WALKER BOOK BELONGS TO:

_____

_____

_____

_____

Walker Read Alouds

FRED THE ANGEL

Written by
MARTIN WADDELL

Illustrated by
PATRICK BENSON

WALKER BOOKS
LONDON

*A book for Sarah and Maeve, written
before Francis was thought of*

First published 1989 by
Walker Books Ltd, 87 Vauxhall Walk
London SE11 5HJ

This edition published 1990

Text © 1989 Martin Waddell
Illustrations © 1989 Patrick Benson

Printed in Great Britain by
Richard Clay Ltd, Bungay, Suffolk

British Library Cataloguing in Publication Data
Martin Waddell
Fred the angel.
I. Title   II. Benson, Patrick
823'.914 [J]   PZ7
ISBN 0-7445-0832-0

CONTENTS

THIS BOOK IS ABOUT:

Fred,
who wanted to be
an Angel

Wortsley,
the Chief Inspector
of Angels

Basil,
Wortsley's Bad Brother

Oscar,
the Poetic Angel

Hermione,
the Loveliest Angel
of Them All

Green Barrow,
the Gardening Angel

And featuring,
in a passing
non-appearance,
Schubert
and introducing
Sarah, who saw Fred,
although she wasn't
supposed to be able to
and Maeve,
who didn't

Pink Mum,
the Singing Angel

Bless them all!

"Congratulations, Fred!" Wortsley said.
"You have passed your Angel Exams!"

THE ANGEL
WHO LOST
HIS CLOUD

Fred wanted to be an Angel.

Being an Angel doesn't just *happen*. You have to work at it. You have to be very good for a long time and pass all the Angel Exams, and then you get made into one.

Fred was good, for ages and ages and ages, even on Saturdays. He practised hard on the harp, and he was kind and generous and unselfish and he learned to sing cheerfully, although not always in tune.

One day Wortsley, the Chief Inspector of Angels, called Fred up to his cloud, which was a very special one with a silver lining.

"Congratulations, Fred!" Wortsley said. "You have passed your Angel Exams!"

"Yippee!" cried Fred, throwing his harp up in the air. It went up a long way and hit a passing Saint on the ear.

"Ouch!" said the Saint. "Who threw that harp?"

"Oh, *gosh*!" said Fred. "I'm terribly sorry. It was me!"

"I forgive you," said the Saint. Saints are like that.

"Not a good start, Fred," said Wortsley, with a frown.

"I promise it won't happen again," said Fred.

"See that it doesn't," said Wortsley. "As I was saying, Fred, you have done well in your examinations, apart from your singing, which is terrible!"

"I'm sorry about my singing," said Fred. "I promise I will practise."

"You'll have to," said Wortsley. "For

now, you must stand at the back of the Heavenly Choir and open your mouth, but don't sing. Do you understand?"

"Understood," said Fred.

"No singing then," said Wortsley. "No flying until you've passed your Wings Test, and no harp throwing."

"Certainly no harp throwing," said Fred.

"Before you can become a fully fledged Angel, Fred, you need some practical experience. I'm going to let you out on trial, and see how you get on when you have problems to cope with."

"Oh," said Fred, looking very serious.

"It won't be easy," said Wortsley.

"I know that, Wortsley," said Fred.

"I'm going to start you off tomorrow," said Wortsley. "The question is, what sort of Angel do you want to be?"

"What sorts of Angels are there?" said

Fred, who had been so busy wanting to become an Angel of any sort that he hadn't stopped to think about the details.

"All sorts!" said Wortsley. "Some Angels spend all day Harp Playing and some Angels are on the Keep Heaven Tidy Campaign and some Angels look after Lost Causes and some Angels go around being Generally Helpful, but I had something special in mind for you to begin with."

"That's very kind of you, Wortsley," said Fred.

"Angels are very kind," said Wortsley. "You ought to know that."

"Yes, Wortsley," said Fred.

"I thought we might start you off with Urgent Prayers," said Wortsley.

"Oh!" said Fred. "*Big* Ones?"

"Small Ones," said Wortsley. "Small Prayers are just as important as Big Ones to the person who is doing the praying."

"Small Urgent Prayers, to begin with!" said Fred, happily.

The next morning Wortsley took Fred to the stores and allowed him to pick his Cloud for dashing about on, a pair of Wings to practise with for his Wings Test, a case to carry them in when they weren't in use, and a map of the part of Glasgow where he was to look after Small Urgent Prayers.

"Great!" said Fred, and off he went.

His first job was an Urgent Prayer about Sarah's lost kitten.

Zoom!

Off went Fred on his Cloud until he spied the kitten, which was wandering up the Bearsden Road.

Fred couldn't just zoom down and grab it. That isn't the way Angels do things. He

*Fred had to make sure Sarah's kitten
wasn't run over by a lorry.*

had to rush back to Sarah and make her think it would be a good idea to ask her dad to look for the kitten. *Then* he had to make her dad agree to go out and search, even though he was tired after a hard day at the hospital, and *then* Fred had to make Sarah's dad turn left, not right, at the cross-roads, *and* he had to make sure Sarah's kitten wasn't run over by a lorry.

"Wasn't that lucky, Sarah?" Sarah's dad said when he came home with the kitten.

"Yes, it was!" said Sarah, who had forgotten all about her Small Urgent Prayer in the excitement, but Fred didn't mind. He was only doing his job.

The next Prayer was easy, because Gran wanted Baby Alicia to go to sleep. Normally Fred would have sung to Alicia but Wortsley had said he wasn't allowed to sing, so Fred played his harp instead. Angels' harps are *odd*, and Fred's playing interfered with TV reception. A lot of people got cross and shouted rude things, but Fred, being an Angel, didn't understand the rude things, and he went on playing until Baby Alicia went to sleep.

The next prayer looked easy, but it wasn't. It was from a farmer who wanted rain to make things grow. When Fred went to check the records he found that there was already a Prayer on file from Darren, the Angel who had had the job before him. Little Tom Cosgrave wanted fine weather for his picnic with Catherine and James.

Fred didn't know what to do, so he asked Wortsley.

"When is the picnic?" asked Wortsley.

"Three until five," said Fred.

"Let it rain up to two o'clock, then have sunshine until six, and then it can rain again for the farmer," said Wortsley, and that is what Fred arranged. Angels are very fair about Prayers, and try to get them right, when they can.

The farmer got his rain, and little Tom Cosgrave got sun for his picnic with Catherine and James.

Then Fred got a Prayer for a new doll, which he turned down because the girl had ten already. After that, he got one to stop toothache hurting, which was silly, because the tooth only hurt because it needed filling. If it wasn't filled, it would hurt much more in the end. Next he got half a dozen prayers, one after the other, for Our-Team-to-Score-a-Goal, and he granted them all because they came three-a-side, and that made the result of the football match a draw, three goals each.

By this time Fred was tired out, so he

thought he would zoom back to Heaven for some refreshment. He parked his Cloud outside the Golden Gates and went in for some Wine and Honey and a smile from Hermione, the Loveliest Angel of Them All. When he came out again, his Cloud was *gone*!

"Gone!" gasped Fred, in dismay.

"What's gone?" said Wortsley, who as Chief Inspector of Angels had been fluttering close to Fred most of the morning, although Fred hadn't seen him.

"My Cloud," said Fred. "I left it outside, and now somebody has gone off on it."

"I see," said Wortsley.

"It was a nice one too," said Fred. "I picked that one specially when you showed it to me, because it was pink. There aren't many pink Clouds around."

"I know," said Wortsley.

He knew, because Wortsley had *made* Fred take that particular Cloud, in the same way that Fred *made* Sarah's dad go out to look for the kitten. That is the way that Angels do things.

"Now it is gone!" said Fred.

"What are you going to do about it?" asked Wortsley.

"Go and look for it, I suppose," said Fred, beginning to sound grumpy. Angels shouldn't be grumpy, and Fred knew that, but he was proud of his Cloud and very upset at losing it.

"If that is what you think best, you must do it," said Wortsley. "Borrow one of the old grey clouds from the store."

Fred took one of the grey clouds. It was tatty round the edges and not in the least pink. It wasn't very fast, but it was the best of a bad bunch. He went off on it to

*Oscar zoomed off on his cloud without
so much as trying to be helpful.*

hunt for his cloud.

He went round the Gorbals, and through Cardonnel, and over to Ibrox, and round Parkhead, but he couldn't find his Cloud anywhere.

Fred went back to Heaven for a quick hymn to cheer himself up, and then he met his friend Oscar, the Poetic Angel, and he asked Oscar if Oscar had seen a missing pink Cloud.

"Hmm," said Oscar. "Where did you get it?"

"Wortsley gave it to me," said Fred.

"Oh, *did* he!" said Oscar, and he zoomed off on his Cloud to give a poetry reading from his very own book of poems, without so much as trying to be helpful.

"Very badly behaved for an Angel, I must say!" grumbled Fred.

"Do you think so?" said Wortsley, popping up from just behind Fred yet again.

"Just like a Poet!" said Fred. "Head in the clouds! No time to be helpful."

"Maybe he was trying to help by *not* helping, Fred," said Wortsley.

"How can not helping be helpful?" asked Fred.

"Perhaps he knew it was important for you to think it out yourself," said Wortsley.

"I have thought about it," said Fred impatiently. "I have been dashing all over Glasgow thinking about it."

"Do you do your best thinking dashing about?" asked Wortsley, and Fred shook his head. "I suggest you try again. I'm afraid if you can't think it out for yourself, you're going to fail your First Test."

"Oh dear!" said Fred. "Oh dear, oh dear, oh dear!" And he rushed off to look for his Cloud again.

"Don't rush, Fred!" called Wortsley.

"Sorry," said Fred.

Fred went on very slowly. He had another look around Glasgow, checking out the airport and the railway station and Sauchiehall Street. It was past six o'clock by now and raining, just as Fred had arranged for the farmer, so there were plenty of clouds. But none of them were pink.

"I'm going to fail my First Test, and then Wortsley won't let me be an Angel after all," Fred thought, miserably.

"I must cheer myself up," he said. Angels are supposed to be cheerful, not miserable, so Fred went off to Tom Cosgrave's house, and the farmer's house and Baby Alicia's house and the footballers' houses and Sarah's house to cheer himself up, but it didn't work.

"They're all so happy now! I wish it was

23

as easy for me!" Fred muttered.

"Why is it easy for them?" asked Wortsley, putting in another of his surprise appearances by Fred's side. Fred was perched on the top branch of the tall tree in Sarah's garden, and Wortsley almost knocked him off it.

"When they had problems, all they had to do was pray, and an Angel popped down to help them!" said Fred.

"Ahem! Ahem!" said Wortsley, and he started whistling and looking at the sky.

"Pray?" asked Fred. "It wouldn't work, would it?"

"If you don't believe in Prayers, nobody will!" said Wortsley, rather impatiently.

"Just a little one, a quickie?" said Fred, doubtfully.

"Speed is not important," said Wortsley.

So Fred tried a Prayer...

. . .and the Prayer *worked*!

"One pink Cloud," said Wortsley as the Cloud came drifting down to the top of the tree in Sarah's garden.

"My Cloud!" said Fred.

"Rather good, that, I thought!" said Wortsley. "I may be Chief Inspector of Angels, but I can still do my bit when it comes to Small Urgent Prayers, if requested!"

"Wortsley," said Fred nervously. "Does . . .does this mean I've failed?"

"No!" said Wortsley. "You've passed! No one can be an Angel who doesn't believe in Prayer! You can continue as usual, Fred!"

"Oh, Wortsley!" said Fred delightedly. "Thank you very, very much!"

"Don't thank me," said Wortsley. "Just say a little Prayer!"

There was a flutter of Wings as
the Heavenly Choir backed away.

THE
EXTRA-SPECIAL
ANGEL

"Once more, Fred!" said Wortsley, waving his golden Conductor's baton. Wortsley was examining Pink Mum's singing class.

"Fah, soh, doh, ray!" sang Fred shrilly, and the rest of the Heavenly Choir covered their ears with their wings, knowing what was coming next.

"Better stop, I think, Fred!" said Wortsley hurriedly, but he was too late.

"*Meeeeeeeeeeeeeee!*" squeaked Fred, completely out of tune.

There was a flutter of Wings as the Heavenly Choir backed away.

"I think, just for the moment, you should go off and practise a long, long way from everybody else, so that we can't hear you," said Wortsley.

"Yes, Wortsley," said Fred, and off he went, feeling very glum. Fred couldn't help being a bad singer, he just was one.

He went to his room.

When he got there, he found a big parcel propped up against his bed. It was addressed:

FRED

HEAVEN

GHQ1

GHQ1 was the post code. Everybody in Heaven uses the post code.

Fred opened the parcel. There was a mirror inside, with a card attached to it:

WINNER

ANGEL OF THE YEAR AWARD.

"Who won it?" Fred said.

"Look and see," said a voice.

"Wortsley?" said Fred, looking round him and expecting the Chief Inspector of Angels to pop up from somewhere to congratulate him.

"Go on," said the voice. "Look in the mirror."

Fred propped the mirror up on the end of his bed.

"Me!" he cried. "I won!"

"Mirror, mirror on the wall ..." began the Voice.

"Who is the fairest of us all?" finished Fred.

"Fred is," said the Voice.

"No I'm not!" Fred said. "Hermione is!" Hermione was the loveliest Angel Fred had ever seen. Nobody was lovelier than Hermione.

"Look in the mirror again," prompted the Voice.

Fred looked.

"Handsome, aren't you?" the Voice said.

Fred considered. "A bit," he said, doubt-fully.

"Very," said the Voice.

"W-e-l-l ..." Fred said.

"And dashing, and good, and brave," said the Voice.

"But I'm still not the Winner of the Angel of the Year Award!" Fred objected. "I can't be. I'm not even a proper Angel yet. I can't fly, and I can't sing."

"Who says you can't sing?" said the Voice.

"Wortsley," said Fred.

"And *what* does Wortsley know about singing?" asked the Voice.

Fred pricked up his ears. The Voice

*Fred looked in the mirror.
"Handsome, aren't you?" the Voice said.*

sounded like Wortsley's, but it couldn't be Wortsley, could it?

"It's my award, and you've won it!" said the Voice, impatiently.

Fred sprang forward, and pulled open the wardrobe door.

Someone who looked very like Wortsley was curled up inside, hanging from a coat hanger. It was Wortsley's Bad Brother, Basil.

"What are you doing in my wardrobe, Basil?" Fred demanded.

"I've come to congratulate you, Fred!" said Basil, unhooking himself from the coat hanger, and climbing out of the wardrobe. "Word gets around, you know! I've been told that you've passed all your exams!"

"Except my Wings Test," said Fred.

"No trouble at all, to an Angel like you," said Basil.

"And I can't sing!" said Fred.

"Ah," said Basil. "That's what they told you, is it?"

"Yes, it is," said Fred.

"Let me hear you sing, Fred," said Basil, and he sat down on the end of the bed.

Fred looked uneasy. Basil was Wortsley's Bad Brother, and Fred knew the rules. No one was supposed to speak to Basil, except to tell him to go away, and he had to go when an Angel told him to. Fred was supposed to tell Basil to go, but . . .

"Doh! Ray! Me!" sang Fred.

"Perfect!" said Basil. "Beautiful voice, Fred!"

"Fah! Soh! Lah! Te! Doooh!" squeaked Fred.

"Absolutely first rate!" said Basil. "I thought it would be. It isn't the first time this has happened, you know."

33

"Well," said Basil. "It's the Heavenly
Choir, you see! Out of tune, Fred! Always!"

"What?" said Fred.

"Well," said Basil. "It's the Heavenly Choir, you see! Out of tune, Fred! Always!"

"But ... but ..." Fred said, because he thought the Choir sang very nicely.

"Then when someone with a *real* voice, someone who *can* sing comes along ... *they* all say he's out of tune! If *they* said he was *in* tune *they'd* all be *out* of tune themselves, wouldn't they?"

"Are you sure?" said Fred.

"Yes," said Basil. "Wortsley and Pink Mum let them get away with it!"

"I ... I don't think I believe you, Basil," said Fred. "Go away!"

And Basil had to go away, because Fred had told him to.

"Doh! Ray! Me!" sang Fred. It sounded *very* good.

Perhaps Basil was *right*. And Wortsley and Pink Mum were *wrong*.

Fred looked in the mirror.

"I am rather handsome," he thought. "But I'm too modest to say so!"

Then he hopped up onto his bed and pulled the carrying case containing his Wings off the top of his wardrobe. His Wings were soft and downy, made of the very best feathers. They gleamed glossily. They were brand new, because Fred had never flown with them. He wasn't allowed to fly without proper supervision.

Fred put his Wings on, and stood in front of the mirror, flapping them.

"Whee!" Fred said. "This is me, flying like a proper Angel!" He ran around the room, flapping his wings, dipping, bending and soaring like an Angel in full flight.

When he was puffed out, he stopped.

"Winner of the Angel of the Year Award!" he thought. "Me! Whoopee!" and he went off to find someone to tell about it.

He went to the canteen, where he met his friend Oscar.

"Bless you, Oscar!" he said. (*Bless you* is what Angels say when they mean *hello*.)

"Bless you, Fred," said Oscar. "I wouldn't bother going into the canteen today if I were you."

"Why not?" said Fred.

"It is peaches and cream and strawberries and jelly and ice-cream *again*," said Oscar, in a cross voice.

"Complaining, Oscar?" said Wortsley, appearing from nowhere, just beside the halo stand at the canteen door.

"No, Wortsley," said Oscar.

"Now you're telling lies, Oscar!" said Wortsley.

"Yes, Wortsley," said Oscar.

"See that it doesn't happen again!" said Wortsley, and he disappeared as swiftly as he had come.

"Yah! Booh!" said Fred, sticking out his tongue in the direction of the halo stand.

"You shouldn't say 'Yah! Booh!' to Wortsley, Fred!" said Oscar.

"Wortsley doesn't know everything!" said Fred. "He's pretending I can't sing, and I know I can!"

"Can you?" said Oscar.

"I'm really the best singer there is!" said Fred. "All the Heavenly Choir pretend I can't sing. They're all jealous because I can sing in tune and they can't."

"I see," said Oscar.

"I'm Angel of the Year, I am!" said Fred, boastfully.

"Are you *sure*, Fred?" said Oscar.

"Yes," said Fred. "Of course, if you don't believe me, Oscar ..."

"I'm a Poet, Fred," said Oscar hurriedly. "I haven't time to argue with you!" And he flapped his Wings and rose up in the air, flying off to Edinburgh to compose a poem about spring and flowers and Wortsley.

"I bet I'm a better poet than Oscar is!" Fred said to himself.

And he made up a poem.

FRED'S POEM
Fred is handsome
Fred is good
Fred does what
An Angel should!
That is why
It is so clear
Fred is the Angel
Of the Year.

*"Parsley and Poetry don't go together!" said
Green Barrow, and he chased Fred with his rake.*

When he had finished it, he went and recited it to Green Barrow, the Gardening Angel.

"Isn't that brilliant, Green Barrow?" said Fred.

"No," said Green Barrow.

"What?" said Fred.

"You're standing on my parsley!" said Green Barrow.

"I'm talking about Poetry!" said Fred loftily.

"And I'm talking about parsley!" said Green Barrow. "Parsley and Poetry don't go together!" and he chased Fred with his rake.

Fred got away, and went back to his Cloud.

Basil was leaning against it.

"Been standing on Green Barrow's parsley, Fred?" said Basil.

"Ye-ye-yes!" panted Fred.

41

"Best thing for it!" said Basil. "Stamping down does parsley a world of good, this time of the year."

"That's right," said Fred.

"I suppose Green Barrow doesn't know about it," said Basil. "You could try telling him, but I wouldn't bother if I were you. He doesn't like to think anyone knows more about gardening than he does, which of course you do."

"Of course," said Fred.

"Singer! Gardener! There's nothing you can't do, Fred, is there?" said Basil.

"You forgot Poet," said Fred, and he recited his poem for Basil.

"Brilliant!" said Basil. "What a very Extra-Special Angel you are, Fred!"

"Yes, I am," said Fred.

He went off to tell everybody how Extra-Special he was, but all the Angels were busy, so in the end he got out his Cloud and zoomed off down to Bearsden. Fred often went there, because it was the scene of his first success, with Sarah's kitten, and he liked to be reminded of it.

Sarah was playing in her playroom, and Fred perched in the big tree with the squirrels at the back of the garden and watched her.

Sarah looked out of the window, and waved at him.

Fred almost dropped out of his tree. Ordinary people aren't supposed to be able to see Angels.

He went down to the playroom.

"Hello," said Sarah. "You're an Angel, aren't you?"

"I'm ... well, sort of!" Fred stuttered, with part of him wondering about explaining that he wasn't a proper Angel yet, and

*"You didn't know I could see you,
did you?" said Sarah. "Well, I can."*

part of him wondering about not being seen.

"You didn't know I could see you, did you?" said Sarah. "Well, I can."

"Most people can't," said Fred.

"Most people aren't me!" said Sarah. "I've seen you floating about on your Cloud lots and lots of times."

"Have you?" said Fred.

"Why can't you fly?" said Sarah.

"I can!" said Fred.

"You can't," said Sarah. "You haven't any Wings. You're not a proper Angel!"

"Yes I am," said Fred. "Only ... I didn't bring my Wings, so I can't just now."

"What can you do?"

"I can sing," said Fred.

"Go on then," said Sarah.

"Doh! Ray! *Meeeeeeeee!*" squeaked Fred.

Sarah stuffed her fingers in her ears.

"Wasn't that nice singing?" said Fred, not very hopefully.

"No, it wasn't," said Sarah. "What else can you do?"

"I know about gardens," said Fred. "I know parsley needs stamping down, this time of the year."

"No it doesn't," said Sarah.

"Yes it does!" said Fred.

"My daddy won the Parsley Prize at Our Show!" said Sarah. "He never stamps on his parsley!"

"Oh," said Fred.

"What else can you do?" demanded Sarah.

"Listen to this," said Fred, his chest swelling with pride, and he recited his poem.

"Fred is handsome,
Fred is good
Fred does what
An Angel should!
That is why
It is so clear
Fred is the Angel
Of the Year."

"That's a very silly, boastful poem," said
Sarah.

"Oh!" said Fred. "Do you think so?"

"Yes, I do," said Sarah. "Whoever wrote
it was rather a stuck-up, unpleasant person,
I would say."

"Would you?" said Fred.

"Did *you* write it?" asked Sarah.

"Ye . . . *no!*" said Fred. "I never did. I
don't . . . I don't write Poetry, actually."

"You don't really do anything much,

do you, Fred?" said Sarah.

"I will, when I'm a proper Angel and get my halo," said Fred.

"Will you get one, do you think?" asked Sarah, doubtfully.

"Well," Fred said. "Basil says I will. Basil says I'm an Extra-Special Angel! Basil says I can do anything."

There was a long silence.

"Did Basil say you could sing?" asked Sarah.

Fred nodded.

"And do gardening? And write poems?"

"Yes," said Fred, sadly.

"And you've been going round boasting about it, haven't you?" said Sarah. "I don't think Angels are supposed to boast."

"I should never have listened to Basil!" said Fred. "Basil is bad! Now I've annoyed Oscar, and Green Barrow, and Wortsley, and all the Angels in the Heavenly Choir, if they've heard about it! Oh dear, what shall I do?"

"Apologise!" said Sarah. "That's what I'm supposed to do when I'm rude to people."

"Angels are never rude!" said Fred.

"Y-e-s," said Sarah. "But boasting is a way of being rude, Fred."

Fred thought about it.

"How can I apologise?" he asked Sarah.

"Don't know," said Sarah.

Fred thought about it.

Then, "I know! I know!" he said, and he zoomed off on his Cloud back to Heaven.

"Wortsley," said Oscar. "Wortsley, what is that up there?"

Wortsley looked up.

High above their heads a Cloud was

dashing about, leaving vapour trail patterns behind it.

"It is spelling something," said Wortsley. "It is spelling: 'I-A-M-S'."

"Iams?" said Oscar. "What does Iams mean?"

" 'O-R-R-Y,' " said Wortsley, following the Cloud with his eyes.

"Orry?" said Oscar.

" 'I am sorry'," Wortsley spelt out.

"What for?" said Oscar, because Wortsley didn't usually apologise for anything. Of course, he didn't have to, usually.

"The Cloud is spelling 'I am sorry'," said Wortsley.

Oscar spelt out the rest of the message. " 'Signed Fred'," he read out. "You were right! He jolly well should be sorry too, after all that showing off!"

"*It is spelling something,*" *said*
Wortsley. "*It is spelling:* '*I-A-M-S*'."

"Some Angels have very short memories, Oscar,"
said Wortsley. "Yes, Wortsley," said Oscar.

"Basil got him with the old Angel of the Year Trick," said Wortsley. "You may remember he got you with it too, Oscar, not so long ago!"

"Oh," said Oscar. "Did he?"

"Some Angels have very short memories, Oscar," said Wortsley.

"Yes, Wortsley," said Oscar.

"Fred will make a very fine Angel indeed, some day," said Wortsley. "But don't tell him I said so, will you?"

And Oscar didn't!

"Do you think I'll ever be a proper Angel,
Green Barrow?" asked Fred.

THE
FALLING
ANGEL

"Do you think I'll ever be a proper Angel, Green Barrow?" asked Fred.

Fred and Green Barrow were out in the Heavenly Gardens, gathering up the fallen leaves.

"Yes," said Green Barrow. "Keep raking!"

Fred put his head down and raked and raked as fast as he could for at least half a minute.

"I'm never going to listen to Wortsley's Bad Brother Basil again!" he said. "Do you know why, Green Barrow?"

"No," said Green Barrow. "Keep raking, Fred!"

"Of course I will," said Fred, leaning on his rake. "I was telling you about Basil. Basil is so bad that he made me believe I was already the best Angel there is. And I'm not a proper Angel at all yet, am I, Green Barrow?"

"No," said Green Barrow, raking round Fred's feet.

"But I will be, won't I?"

"Not if you keep talking instead of raking!" said Green Barrow, grimly.

"I'm terribly sorry, Green Barrow," said Fred. "Now as I was saying, Basil is bad, and he – "

"Oh, go away, Fred!" said Green Barrow. "You're wasting my time!"

Fred went away, feeling very upset.

"No good at flying! Talk too much!" Fred muttered, walking across the grass to a shady place, where he could be alone.

"I'll never be a proper Angel!" Fred thought, and then he heard a sweet sound, which reminded him of summertime and flowers and mountain streams and butterflies and rice puddings. Most of all it reminded him of rice puddings, which were his favourite puddings. Almost anything that was good and pure and sweet reminded Fred of rice puddings.

Fred tiptoed round the rose bushes, following the sound of the soft, sad music.

"Aha!" he cried, catching sight of the musician. It was Hermione. Hermione was Fred's favourite Angel. She was honey-brown all over, soft dark eyes and shiny black hair and her robes were whiter than anybody else's in Heaven. She was sitting on the grassy bank above the Lily Pond, softly plucking the strings of her harp.

The music she was making was so soft

and gentle that Fred didn't interrupt her. He sat down on the bank above the Lily Pond and waited until she had finished.

"Bless you, Hermione," said Fred. "That was lovely. You remind me of rice puddings."

"Bless you too, Fred," Hermione said, in a sad little voice, and as she spoke a tear ran down her cheek and plopped onto her harp, where it glistened in the sunlight.

"Hermione!" cried Fred. "What in Heaven is the matter?"

"Nothing," said Hermione, as she got up. "Nothing at all, Fred!"

"Yes there is," said Fred.

"No there isn't," said Hermione, and she turned away and walked down the grassy bank.

SPLOOOOOOOOOOOOOOOOSH!

"Ooooooooooh!" wailed Hermione, who

The music Hermione was making was so soft
and gentle that Fred didn't interrupt her.

"Fred to the rescue!" cried Fred,
surfacing with a weed round his head.

had fallen straight into the Lily Pond.

Fred took one look at the lovely little Angel in the Lily Pond and started to run.

"Have no fear, Fred is here!" he shouted, and dived straight into the Lily Pond to save Hermione from drowning.

SPLOOOOOOOOOOOOOOOOSH!

"Oh gosh!" said Hermione, who had just stood up when Fred *splooooooosh*ed! down.

"Fred to the rescue!" cried Fred, surfacing with a weed round his head. Then he looked round for Hermione. He had landed in the deep bit. Hermione hadn't.

"I've rescued myself, thank you very much," said Hermione, stepping onto the bank and wringing out her robes.

Fred didn't say anything.

He had just remembered that he couldn't swim a stroke.

"My turn to rescue *you*, Fred!" sighed

Hermione, and she held out her harp and helped Fred out of the water, which is the safest way to rescue people, without getting drowned yourself.

"Bless you, Fred, for trying to save me from drowning," Hermione said, and she went away leaving Fred dripping on the bank.

"Very noble, Fred," said Wortsley, popping up from behind the rose bushes.

"Wasn't it?" said Fred, who thought he had behaved rather well.

"Feeling proud, Fred?" said Wortsley.

"Only a little, Wortsley," said Fred, hanging his head. He was supposed to be humble all the time, and often found it difficult.

"Never mind," said Wortsley. "It's not a Big Fault, so long as you don't make a habit of it."

"Yes, Wortsley," said Fred. "But you see, sometimes I can't help it. Then when I'm not being proud, I'm being sad because I can't sing, and I can't fly and – "

"Fred!" said Wortsley, holding up his hand.

"Yes, Wortsley?" said Fred.

"What's an Angel's first job, Fred?"

"Looking After Other People, Wortsley," said Fred. "But if I'm proud, and I can't sing and I can't fly I – "

"Do it, Fred!" said Wortsley, and he disappeared.

"Do it!" Fred told himself firmly. "I must stop thinking of myself, and start helping other people like ... like ..."

"Like Hermione!" Wortsley said, appearing beside him in a flash of bright light, and then disappearing again.

"Thank you, Wortsley," said Fred,

politely, to the spot where Wortsley had been. "I should have thought of that myself. Something is the matter with Hermione. Something made her cry. I must try to help Hermione."

He went looking for Hermione.

The first person he met was Green Barrow.

"Feet!" said Green Barrow, pointing accusingly at a flowerbed.

"Pardon?" said Fred.

"Feet!" said Green Barrow.

Fred looked at the flowerbed. There was a trail of footprints leading right across the middle of it.

"Been standing on my plants again, Fred?" said Green Barrow.

The two Angels looked at the footprints. They were small, dainty footprints, rather damp around the edges. They were

"Feet!" said Green Barrow, pointing
accusingly at a flowerbed.

Oscar bustled on his way,
dripping peaches.

Hermione-like footprints.

"Not yours!" said Green Barrow. "You've got Big Feet!"

"I haven't got Big Feet!" said Fred.

"Haven't you?" said Green Barrow. "Remember my parsley?" And he went back to raking the footprints out of the flowerbed.

"Can't sing! Can't fly! Big Feet!" muttered Fred as he went off to find Hermione.

He looked into the canteen, just as Oscar came running out, covered in peaches and cream.

"Bless you, Oscar!" said Fred. "Why are you covered in peaches and cream?"

"Ask Hermione!" said Oscar, and he bustled on his way, dripping peaches.

"I'm terribly sorry, Oscar!" wailed Hermione, appearing in the doorway clutching a towel. "It was a lovely poem. I didn't mean to throw peaches over you. I ..."

But Oscar had gone.

"Oh dear! Oh dear! Oh, Fred, what shall I do?" cried Hermione.

"What have you *done*?" asked Fred.

"I tripped. Oscar was reading us his poem and I tripped, and my peaches and cream went all over him! I ... I just don't know what to do, Fred. I keep banging into things ..."

"Like Lily Ponds?" asked Fred.

"Yes," Hermione sniffed.

"And walking across flowerbeds?"

"Did I?" asked Hermione. "I didn't see it! I've been tumbling and tripping all day. And Basil says – "

"You're not supposed to talk to Wortsley's Bad Brother Basil!" said Fred, sternly.

"I didn't! I didn't! But he talked to me, before I told him to go away. He called me the Falling Angel. And he's right. I keep tripping and falling! I don't know what to do, Fred."

"Come into the canteen and have some peaches and cream," said Fred. "Or strawberries! The strawberries are very good today, I believe."

"Bless you, Fred, and thank you very much for being nice to me after your ducking," said Hermione. "But I couldn't eat peaches and cream or strawberries just now. I think I'll go home and lie down and be sad."

And off she went.

"Ha, ha, ha!" said Basil. "Not much good at helping Hermione, are you, Fred? Not much good at anything!"

"Go away, Basil!" said Fred, and Basil had to go away.

But Basil was right. Fred hadn't done

much good so far. He didn't know what to do to cheer up Hermione, and so he did what he always did when he was stuck, and zoomed off on his Cloud down to Bearsden.

Sarah was having her tea.

Fred tied his Cloud to the big tree and knocked politely on the window, and she let him in. He settled on top of the bookcase.

"Bless you, Sarah," he said.

"Bless you too, Angel," said Sarah.

"My name is Fred, Sarah," said Fred.

"May I call you Fred, Fred?" asked Sarah, politely.

"Just Fred," said Fred.

"Good," said Sarah. "Now tell me what you have been doing today."

And Fred told her about all the lost things he had helped people find and all the good things he had made people think of doing and how busy he had been.

"Very good, Angel, I mean *Fred*," said Sarah. "My dad is good too."

"What does your dad do?" Fred asked politely.

"He works in the hospital," said Sarah. "He looks after people's eyes."

"Does he?" said Fred.

"Yes," said Sarah. "My dad says if he didn't look after people's eyes they wouldn't be able to see properly and they would walk around bumping into things and falling over, but my dad makes sure that that doesn't happen."

"Does he?" said Fred, suddenly sounding very interested. "What does your dad do for them?"

"He gives them glasses," said Sarah.

"Oh! Oh! Oooooooh!" said Fred, and off he zoomed, without even remembering to say goodbye to Sarah, who didn't mind, because she understood that something important must have come up that needed attending to immediately.

"What pretty glasses, Fred!" said Hermione, trying them on. They were bright blue with little jewels on them that winked and glittered in the sun. They were the most beautiful and dainty glasses that Hermione had ever seen.

"Now you won't fall over any more, Hermione," said Fred. "You'll be able to see perfectly."

"Bless you, Fred! Bless you very much!" said Hermione, happily.

"Bless Sarah," said Fred. "She thought of it."

"One Helping Test, passed!" said Wortsley, popping up from behind Hermione's sofa. "Well done, Fred!"

And Hermione gave Fred a Special Congratulations Kiss.

It was lovely, and reminded him of rice
puddings.

"You're light as a feather, Fred!
Light as a feather!" Pink Mum said.

THE
WINGS
TEST

"One, two, three, and *flap!*" sang Pink Mum. "*And* one, two, three, and *flap! And* one, two, three, and *flap!*"

Fred was skipping round the Flying Control Room one-two-three-and-flapping when Pink Mum told him to, but he wasn't very good at it and Pink Mum was getting cross.

"Do concentrate on your flapping, Fred!" she said. "Now, I'll begin again, shall I?" And she played the first three notes on her piano, which meant that Fred had to begin skipping.

"You're light as a feather, Fred! Light as a feather!" Pink Mum said. "Now! One, two, three and *flap*! One, two, three, *flap*!"

Fred sprang lightly into the air, flapped and fell down on his bottom.

"Ouch!" he said.

"We're not flapping, Fred, are we?" said Pink Mum, and she stopped playing the piano. "This will never do! Only a day to go to your Wings Test and you are still one-two-three-flapping, with hardly any lift-off!"

"I'm very sorry, Pink Mum," said Fred.

"Light as a feather, Fred! Light as a feather! Just jump in the air, flap your wings, and you'll float away!" said Pink Mum, not very hopefully.

She sprang into the air and flew round the Flying Control Room above Fred's head, just to show him how it was done. Then she glided down to Fred and took him by the hand.

"One, two, three, *flap*! Fred," she said,

encouragingly.

They floated up to the ceiling with Fred flapping his wings for all he was worth, and Pink Mum keeping up a gentle rhythm.

"I'm flying!" cried Fred. "I'm flying!" and he flapped like mad.

"Of course you are," said Pink Mum. "All it needs is a little practice, just like riding a bicycle."

"Wheeeeeeeeeee!" cried Fred. "I'm a Super Flier. I can fly anywhere! I can ..."

Pink Mum let go of his hand.

"... fly better than almost anybody!" Fred said.

"Can't I?" Fred said.

And then he noticed that Pink Mum had glided down to her piano stool again, and wasn't holding his hand.

"Aaaaaah!" Fred cried, flapping his wings despairingly and heading down in

*Fred's head came out of the piano case,
where the keyboard would usually be.*

a dive.

CRUUUUUUUUUMP!

Fred crash landed.

SPROOOOOOOOOOOOOOONGGGGG!

He not only crash landed, but he landed crash in the middle of Pink Mum's piano. Pink Mum and her piano stool went over in a pile on the floor, and Fred disappeared inside the wrecked piano.

"My piano!" cried Pink Mum. "You've wrecked it!"

Fred's head came out of the piano case, where the keyboard would usually be. He was covered in bits of broken piano.

"Sorry!" he said.

"Never mind, Fred," said Pink Mum, which shows what a kind Angel she was, because she had had her piano for ages and ages and she loved it very much. Just at that moment she didn't love Fred very much, but she didn't let it show because she was a very good Angel.

"I'll fix it, Pink Mum!" Fred said, struggling out of the piano. He was afraid that Pink Mum would tell Wortsley what he had done, and Wortsley would be cross with him, and wouldn't let him take his Wings Test. If he couldn't pass his Wings Test he could never be a proper Angel.

"That's very good of you, Fred," said Pink Mum, and she went off to get her hair done and forget all about Fred and his problems.

Fred set about fixing the piano.

It wasn't as easy as it looked.

He got all the pieces lined up on the floor, the black notes and the white notes and the bits of wire and the broken wood. He borrowed a hammer and nails from Green Barrow's store and he nailed the broken wood together. Then he started on the wires.

"Trouble, Fred?" asked Oscar.

"Bless you, Oscar," said Fred. "Are you any good at fixing pianos?"

"No," said Oscar, who had come out with his notebook to compose another poem about Wortsley, and wasn't going to get himself mixed up in piano fixing. "Why don't you ask Schubert?"

So Fred went to ask Schubert, but Schubert was very busy finishing his Unfinished Symphony and couldn't come.

"Oh dear!" said Fred. "One day before my Wings Test! I should be practising and instead I have this rotten old piano to fix."

"Who broke it, Fred?" asked Wortsley, popping up from behind Fred in his usual way, and giving poor Fred quite a turn. Wortsley had a way of being everywhere at once without you knowing he was there.

"I broke it, Wortsley," said Fred. "But I didn't mean to. Now I am in awful trouble! I promised Pink Mum I would fix her piano but I've got to practise flying for my Wings Test tomorrow and I can't practise flying and fix the piano at the same time and I don't know how to fix the piano anyway, because I am not very good at music."

"And what do Angels do when they are in trouble?" said Wortsley, sounding faintly bored.

"Pray, Wortsley," said Fred.

"One of your quickies?" asked Wortsley.

"Will a quickie do?" asked Fred.

"Perfectly adequate, so long as you mean it," said Wortsley, and he disappeared.

So Fred said a Prayer . . .

. . . and nothing happened.

He had expected an Angelic piano tuner

to come floating down on a Cloud, but no-body did.

"Bother!" said Fred. "Are you there, Wortsley? Are you listening? Nobody has answered my Prayer, Wortsley!"

"Bless you, Fred!" said Hermione, floating daintily down into the Flying Control Room. "What is the matter?"

"Wortsley said I only had to pray and I'd get this piano fixed and I haven't time to fix it myself because it is my Wings Test tomorrow and I prayed and nobody came."

"I came," said Hermione.

Fred looked at her. She was sweet and brown and lovely, positively the most rice pudding Angel in the whole of Heaven. She looked like the answer to an Angel's Prayer, but ...

"I don't think you could manage it, Hermione, thanks all the same," said Fred.

"Fixing pianos is man's work."

"Is it?" said Hermione.

"Yes, it is," said Fred.

"I'll sit and watch you do it then, shall I?" said Hermione sweetly, and she sat down on Fred's Wings' case to watch.

Fred got his hammer, nails, screwdriver, pliers and tuning fork. He set to work.

"This way?" he thought. "Or that?"

"Or ... or ..."

"Try in there, Fred," suggested Hermione.

Fred tried, and it worked.

"I think that that bit goes on top, Fred," said Hermione.

"No," said Fred. "It doesn't screw."

"Just lend me the screwdriver a minute," said Hermione, and with a few deft twists of her dainty fingers she tightened up the screw.

"I'll sit and watch you do it then,
shall I?" said Hermione sweetly.

"There," she said.

"Bless you, Hermione," said Fred.

Then Hermione straightened out the wires and fixed them to the frame, and got the notes in the right order and tuned them, and played "One, Two, Three, *Flap*!" on them.

"Finished," she said. "Well done, Fred."

"I didn't do it," said Fred. "You did!"

"That's what friends are for, Fred," said Hermione, and she flapped her wings and flew away before Fred had a chance to think of anything else that needed doing.

Like Flying Lessons.

The Wings Test was only a day away.

Fred stood where he was, and flapped.

Nothing happened.

"I need confidence! I need practice!" he thought.

"Would you like me to play the piano for you, Fred?" asked Basil, putting in a surprise appearance at the piano stool.

Fred knew that he wasn't supposed to speak to Wortsley's Bad Brother, but he did need someone to play the piano, so that he could practise.

He was still debating whether to say, "Yes please, Basil," or "Go away, Basil," when Basil flexed his fingers and played.

Basil was a very good piano player, New Orleans trained.

"One, two, three, *flap!*" sang Basil, and Fred skipped three times, and flapped obediently. "That's very good, Fred," said Basil, although Fred had only risen a foot or two from the floor. "Now do it again!"

This time, Basil played a little quicker. One-two-*three-flap!* One-*two-three-flap!* *One-two-three-flap!*

*Fred sat down on the floor, gasping with
exhaustion after all his quick flapping.*

"Now you're getting the idea, Fred!" said Basil. "I'll jazz things up a bit, shall I?"

And he one-two-three-flapped even quicker. Faster and faster and faster, so that Fred's wings were a blur as he tried to keep pace.

Faster, and faster, and faster.

"Go away, Basil!" said Wortsley, suddenly appearing on the end of the piano. Wortsley used his flash of blue light to appear with, something he only did when he was cross. "You're getting poor Fred into a flap!"

Basil slunk away.

Fred sat down on the floor, gasping with exhaustion after all his quick flapping. "You'll never learn by listening to Basil, Fred!" said Wortsley. "I thought you'd learned that lesson. First the Angel of the Year Award, and now this!"

Then Wortsley disappeared.

"I'll never learn to fly!" thought Fred, miserably. Fred's trouble was that he couldn't get off the ground in the first place. "If I could get up high, I could glide down, and try a little flap on the way!" he thought. "How could I get up high?"

He remembered the tall tree at the back of Sarah's garden. It was a very tall tree.

"I'll just go and look at it," Fred thought.

He zoomed off to Bearsden on his Cloud.

Sarah was standing at the window watching the rain falling, and wondering if it would snow for Christmas. She saw Fred zooming into her garden, and waved.

"Who are you waving at, Sarah?" asked her mum.

"My Angel," said Sarah.

"Where?" said Mum, going to the window.

"There," said Sarah. "He's at the top of our tree."

Sarah's mum looked out, but she couldn't see anybody.

"What is your Angel up our tree for?" she asked Sarah.

"I don't know," said Sarah.

Fred was on the highest branch.

He stood very still, with his arms straight out, and then he took two skips ... One, two ... and a third one ... three ... and he flapped ... flap ... and stepped off the branch.

Flap-flap-flap-flap-flap-flap-flap-flap-flap-flap-flap-flap-flap-flap-flap-flap

FLOP!

*Fred landed head first
in a pile of wet leaves!*

Fred landed head first in a pile of wet leaves!

Fred got up.

He had leaves in his ears, and leaves stuck up his nose. His lovely Wings were straggly and wet. "Ooooooh!" he moaned sadly.

He saw Sarah standing at the playroom window, and he decided to go and talk to her, because he needed comforting. Even Angels need comforting from time to time, especially when they have wet leaves stuck up their noses.

"Do you like jumping off trees, Angel Fred?" asked Sarah.

"No," said Fred, but he told her about his Wings Test, and how much he needed to practise.

"Did you hurt yourself when you fell off our tree?" asked Sarah.

"Of course not," said Fred, with dignity.

"I didn't fall. I was practising flapping."

"It looked like falling to me," said Sarah.

"Felt like it too!" muttered Fred, with a sniff. "If only I could find some way of getting up in the air without hurting myself . . ."

"I know!" said Sarah. "I know!"

And she showed Fred her trampoline.

"You just bounce on that," said Fred. "I don't see how it helps."

"Let me show you how to do it," said Sarah.

And she bounced, and bounced . . . higher . . . and higher . . . and higher!

"If you bounced with your wings on, you could flap them!" Sarah said.

"Yes!" said Fred. "You're right, I could."

Fred stood on the trampoline.

He bounced.

He flapped.

He bounced.

He flapped.

He bounced.

He flapped.

He bounced.

He flapped, and *flapped*.

He bounced.

He flapped, and *flapped*, and *flapped*.

He bounced.

He flapped, and *flapped*, and *flapped* and *flapped*!

He bounced.

He flapped, and *flapped*, and *flapped*, and *flapped*, and *flapped*, and *flapped*, and *flapped*, and *flapped* and then he ...

F L E W!

"Yippee! I can fly!" Fred cried.

And that is what Pink Mum said to him

Wortsley flew down to Bearsden himself,
for a little quiet trampolining.

next day, after she had examined him for his Wings Test.

"You can fly, Fred!" said Pink Mum. "I never thought you'd do it, but you can fly!" And she pinned his Golden Flyer's Rosette on the shoulder of his robe.

"Well done, Fred!" said Hermione and Oscar and Green Barrow. Basil only scowled.

Wortsley said nothing. He knew all about Sarah's trampoline, and how Fred had got in the last-minute flying practice which allowed him to pass his test. Wortsley knew, but he said nothing. He waited until Fred and the others had nipped off to the canteen to celebrate, and then he flew down to Bearsden himself, for a little quiet trampolining.

Even a Chief Inspector of Angels has to have a little fun sometimes!

*Sarah blew the flute and wakened
her little baby sister, Maeve.*

SARAH'S
CHRISTMAS

It was Christmas Day!

Sarah woke up and there, at the end of her bed, was her stocking.

"Ooooooh!" she said, and she bounced down her bed and grabbed it.

There were new mittens inside, and a scarf, and an orange, and some chocolate money, and a book about kittens and a flute.

Sarah blew the flute and wakened her little baby sister, Maeve. Maeve only had a tiny stocking, because she was a tiny baby. There were sweeties in it, and a doll, and mittens.

"Just like mine!" said Sarah.

"Mine!" said Maeve, bouncing up and down in her cot. All the bouncing and flute playing made so much noise that Sarah's dad had to come up and see what was happening.

"Oh, look!" said Sarah, suddenly.

There was a trail of golden dust leading from the end of Sarah's bed, where her stocking had been, to the end of Maeve's cot, where her stocking had been, and on to the bedroom chair, where somebody had been sitting. You could tell that somebody had been sitting there, because the chair was covered in golden dust, and the same somebody had eaten the biscuits that Sarah had left for him, and finished the orange juice!

"Santa Claus!" gasped Sarah, touching the golden dust, which made her hand golden too.

"He must have come down the chimney!" said Sarah's dad.

"Don't be silly," said Sarah. "We haven't got a chimney!"

Sarah's mum helped Sarah to follow the trail of gold right round the room and out of the door, where it stopped on the landing.

"Where did he go to?" asked Sarah's mum.

"The roof-space!" said Sarah. "He came through the trap door!"

"You're *probably* right," said Dad.

"But how did he get *into* the roof-space?" asked Sarah.

Sarah's dad looked at Sarah's mum, and Sarah's mum looked at Sarah's dad, and he shrugged. "Don't know, Sarah!" he said.

"Maybe there's a hole in the roof," said Sarah.

"I expect that's it," said Mum.

"Presents time, I think!" said Dad.

Sarah got a big doll, much bigger than the little one in Maeve's stocking, and a book called *Famous Fairy Tales* and sweeties and two jigsaw puzzles and a pair of skates and a crash helmet.

Maeve got a new hat, and a coat, and three pairs of red tights, and sweeties, and a pull-along jingle dog, and a musical clock.

Sarah started playing with the clock.

"Mine!" said Maeve, crawling towards it.

"I was only playing with it," said Sarah, putting it behind her back where Maeve couldn't get at it.

"Children!" said Mum. "Remember, it is Christmas."

"Peace!" said Dad. "Everybody has to be good and kind and nice to each other on Christmas Day."

"I know," said Sarah, letting go of the

clock. "Fred told me."

"Fred?" said Dad.

"He's Sarah's Angel," said Mum. "Sarah can see him in the garden. He jumps off trees!"

"He can fly now," said Sarah. "He's passed his Wings Test!"

"Oh," said Dad. "Well done, Fred, wherever you are!"

"He's in Heaven, of course!" said Sarah, who thought her dad was being really silly. Everyone knows Angels live in Heaven.

"I thought you weren't supposed to be able to see Angels," said Dad.

"Well, I can," said Sarah.

"That's because you're very special," said Mum, giving her a hug.

"Maeve can't see Angels!" said Sarah.

"Not yet," said Mum.

They went to church, and had Christmas

dinner and then Mum said she wasn't doing any more work and Dad and Sarah did the dishes and Maeve had her sleep and Sarah went out on the skates wearing her crash helmet and Maeve ate her sweets and Sarah's sweets and was sick and then Maeve went to bed and when Maeve was asleep Sarah went to bed.

"Fred didn't come at *all*!" Sarah complained, when Mum was tucking her up. "He promised he would come to see me on Christmas Day, and he didn't, and I kept some chocolate money for his present!"

"I expect your Angel was kept busy," said Mum. "Christmas must be an Extra-Special Day in Heaven."

"He said he would come to see me!" Sarah objected.

"Tell you what," said Mum. "We'll both say a little prayer to make Fred come."

Sarah went out on the skates
wearing her crash helmet.

Fred appeared on the end of the bed.
"Merry Christmas, Sarah!" he said.

"Yes!" said Sarah.

That's what they did.

"Night-night, Sarah!" said Mum, switching off the light.

Sarah lay very still, counting sheep, waiting for Fred to come zooming down on his cloud.

Then, just as she was about to go to sleep, something happened.

The bedroom lit up with a soft, glowing blue light that spread from the end of Sarah's bed right into the shadows, and made baby Maeve stir in her sleep. Then, there was the sound of gently beating wings, and Fred appeared, on the end of the bed.

"Merry Christmas, Sarah!" Fred said.

"Oh! Oh, Fred! You do look lovely!" said Sarah, and he did.

His robes were gleaming white, and there

was a golden light around his head.

"Is that ... is that ..."

"My Halo," said Fred proudly. "I'm a proper Angel now. I was made one in the Birthday Honours List!"

"Fred!" said Sarah. "Congratulations!"

Then Fred told her all about Christmas in Heaven, and his presents. Wortsley gave him Pink Mum's book *How to Sing* (because his singing was still not *quite* right) and he got a Christmas Rose from Green Barrow and some woolly underpants for night flying from Pink Mum and a book of Oscar's poems from Oscar, and a signed photograph of Wortsley from Basil (with a funny hat inked in, and a red nose crayoned on, and great big ears), and a Christmas kiss from Hermione, which was the present he liked best of all.

"I got you a present, Fred," said Sarah,

*A Christmas kiss from Hermione, which
was the present Fred liked best of all.*

and she gave him the chocolate money from her stocking, which she had saved for him. It had got a bit squashy, under her pillow, but Fred said it was delicious.

"I have something special for you too!" said Fred, and he gave her a large slice of the most gorgeous-looking cake she had ever seen, glittering with decorations, and filled up with peaches and cream and strawberries and cherries and bananas and pineapple and nuts and everything lovely in the world, or elsewhere.

"Oh, thank you very much, Fred!" said Sarah, because it looked scrumptious.

"It is my slice of *The* Birthday Cake," said Fred. "I saved it specially for you, Sarah!"

"Whose Birthday?" asked Sarah.

"You know!" said Fred.

"Oh," said Sarah. *"Christmas!"*

"The Most Special Birthday Cake There Is!" said Fred proudly, and Sarah shared her slice with him, and they were both very happy.

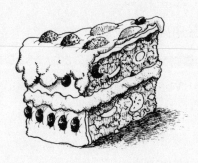

THE
END